How to Analyze the Works of
GEORGE WASHINGTON

by Annie Qaiser

ABDO
Publishing Company

Essential Critiques

How to Analyze the Works of

GEORGE WASHINGTON

by Annie Qaiser

Content Consultant: Aaron J. Little
Department of Writing Studies, University of Minnesota–Twin Cities

Credits

Published by ABDO Publishing Company, PO Box 398166, Minneapolis, MN 55439. Copyright © 2013 by Abdo Consulting Group, Inc. International copyrights reserved in all countries. No part of this book may be reproduced in any form without written permission from the publisher. The Essential Library™ is a trademark and logo of ABDO Publishing Company.

Printed in the United States of America,
North Mankato, Minnesota
112012
012013

THIS BOOK CONTAINS AT LEAST 10% RECYCLED MATERIALS.

Editor: Angela Wiechmann
Series Designer: Marie Tupy

Cataloging-in-Publication Data
Qaiser, Annie.
 How to analyze the works of George Washington / Annie Qaiser.
   p. cm. -- (Essential critiques)
Includes bibliographical references and index.
ISBN 978-1-61783-645-9
1. Washington, George--1732-1799--Criticism and interpretation--Juvenile literature. 2. Presidents--United States--Juvenile literature. I. Title.
973.4--dc14

2012946240

Table of Contents

Chapter 1	Introduction to Critiques	6
Chapter 2	A Closer Look at George Washington	12
Chapter 3	An Overview of Washington's First Inaugural Address	22
Chapter 4	How to Apply Biographical Criticism to Washington's First Inaugural Address	28
Chapter 5	An Overview of "Washington's Advice on Love & Marriage"	40
Chapter 6	How to Apply Feminist Criticism to "Washington's Advice on Love & Marriage"	46
Chapter 7	An Overview of Washington's Farewell Address	56
Chapter 8	How to Apply Historical Criticism to Washington's Farewell Address	64
Chapter 9	An Overview of Washington's Will	74
Chapter 10	How to Apply Moralist Criticism to Washington's Will	84

You Critique It	96
Timeline	98
Glossary	100
Bibliography of Works and Criticism	102
Resources	104
Source Notes	106
Index	110
About the Author	112

Chapter 1

Introduction to Critiques

What Is Critical Theory?

What do you usually do when you read a book or essay or listen to a speech? You probably absorb the specific language style of the work. You also consider the point the speaker or writer is trying to convey. Yet these are only a few of many possible ways of understanding and appreciating a speech or piece of writing. What if you are interested in delving more deeply? You might want to learn more about the writer or speaker and how his or her personal background is reflected in the work. Or you might want to examine what the work says about society—how it depicts the roles of women and minorities, for example. If so, you have entered the realm of critical theory.

Critical theory helps you learn how art, literature, music, theater, film, politics, and other endeavors either support or challenge the way society behaves. Critical theory is the evaluation and interpretation of a work using different philosophies, or schools of thought. Critical theory can be used to understand all types of cultural works.

There are many different critical theories. Each theory asks you to look at the work from a different perspective. Some theories address social issues, while others focus on the writer's or speaker's life or the time period in which the work was created. For example, the critical theory that asks how an author's life affected the work is called biographical criticism. Other common schools of criticism include historical criticism, feminist criticism, psychological criticism, and New Criticism, which examines a work solely within the context of the work itself.

What Is the Purpose of Critical Theory?

Critical theory can open your mind to new ways of thinking. It can help you evaluate a piece of writing or a speech from a new perspective, directing your attention to issues and messages you may not otherwise recognize in a work. For example, applying feminist criticism to an essay may make you aware of female stereotypes perpetuated in the work. Applying a critical theory to a speech helps you learn about the person who gave it or the society that heard it. You can also explore how the work is perceived by current cultures.

How Do You Apply Critical Theory?

You conduct a critique when you use a critical theory to examine and question a work. The theory you choose is a lens through which you can view the work, or a springboard for asking questions

INTRODUCTION TO CRITIQUES

about the work. Applying a critical theory helps you think critically about the work. You are free to question the work and make assertions about it. If you choose to examine an essay using biographical criticism, for example, you want to know how the writer's personal background or education inspired or shaped the work. You could explore why the writer was drawn to the subject. For instance, are there any parallels between points raised in the essay and details from the writer's life?

Forming a Thesis

Ask your question and find answers in the work or other related materials. Then you can create a thesis. The thesis is the key point in your critique. It is your argument about the work based on the tenets, or beliefs, of the theory you are using. For example, if you are using biographical criticism to ask how the writer's life inspired the work, your thesis could be worded as follows: Writer Teng Xiong, raised in refugee camps in Southeast Asia, drew upon her experiences to write the essay "No Home for Me."

How to Make a Thesis Statement

In a critique, a thesis statement typically appears at the end of the introductory paragraph. It is usually only one sentence long and states the author's main idea.

How to Analyze the Works of GEORGE WASHINGTON

Providing Evidence

Once you have formed a thesis, you must provide evidence to support it. Evidence might take the form of examples and quotations from the work itself—such as excerpts from an essay. Articles about the essay or personal interviews with the writer might also support your ideas. You may wish to address what other critics have written about the work. Quotes from these individuals may help support your claim. If you find any quotes or examples that contradict your thesis, you will need to create an argument against them. For instance: Many critics have pointed to the essay "No Home for Me" as detailing only the powerless circumstances Xiong faced. However, in the paragraphs focused on her emigration to the United States, Xiong clearly depicts herself as someone who can shape her own future.

How to Support a Thesis Statement

A critique should include several arguments. Arguments support a thesis claim. An argument is one or two sentences long and is supported by evidence from the work being discussed.

Organize the arguments into paragraphs. These paragraphs make up the body of the critique.

In This Book

In this book, you will read summaries of famous works by President George Washington, each followed by a critique. Each critique will use one theory and apply it to one work. Critical thinking sections will give you a chance to consider other theses and questions about the work. Did you agree with the author's application of the theory? What other questions are raised by the thesis and its arguments? You can also find out what other critics think about each work. Then, in the You Critique It section in the final pages of this book, you will have an opportunity to create your own critique.

> **Look for the Guides**
>
> Throughout the chapters that analyze the works, thesis statements have been highlighted. The box next to the thesis helps explain what questions are being raised about the work. Supporting arguments have been underlined. The boxes next to the arguments help explain how these points support the thesis. Look for these guides throughout each critique.

How to Analyze the Works of GEORGE WASHINGTON

Essential Critiques

From an early age, Washington's leadership skills were valued in military and politics.

Chapter 2

A Closer Look at George Washington

Early Life

George Washington, the first president of the United States of America, was born on February 22, 1732, in Westmoreland County, Virginia. Washington was the son of Augustine Washington and his second wife, Mary Ball Washington.

George grew up on his father's farm and spent much of his time outdoors in the Virginia woods. He was close to his older brother, Lawrence, who was Augustine's son from his first marriage. In 1743, Augustine Washington died suddenly. George's father left most of his funds and estates to his children from his first marriage. George, on the other hand, received only a few hundred acres and ten slaves.

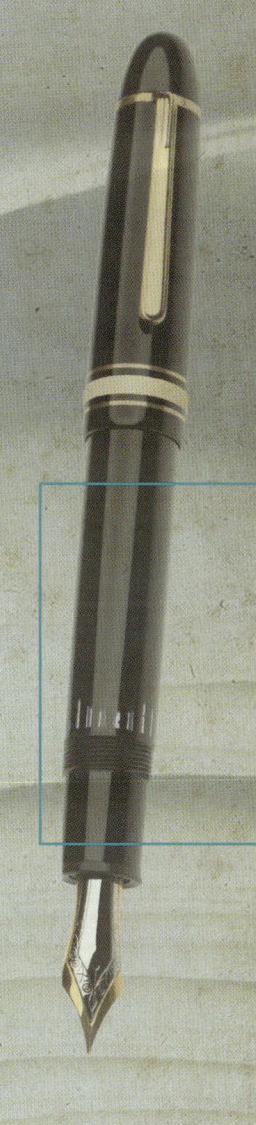

George's formal education ended soon afterward—something that plagued him his entire life. While others of his age and social status obtained a formal education abroad, George did not have the money. Instead, he ran a household, managed a farm, and began a profession.

George greatly respected Lawrence as a father figure. Lawrence, in turn, helped George get his first job, which would launch him on his path to greatness. Lawrence was related by marriage to Lord Fairfax, one of the largest landholders in Virginia. In 1748, when George was 16, he joined the surveying party venturing into Lord Fairfax's lands in the Shenandoah Valley. George gained new skills and indispensable knowledge for his future career in surveying. He proved to be a quick learner and was appointed as a surveyor in Culpeper County in 1749.

New Responsibilities

In 1751, Lawrence became sick with tuberculosis. He traveled to Barbados, an island in the Caribbean Sea, in hopes of improving his health. Washington traveled with him. During this journey, Washington contracted smallpox, which left scars on his face for the rest of his life. Shortly afterward, in 1752, Lawrence died, and Washington inherited his estate, Mount Vernon.

Also in 1752, the governor of Virginia selected Washington to be a lieutenant in the Virginia military. Washington proved to have solid skills and good character for military positions. He launched into prominence during the outbreak of the French and Indian War (1754–1763). Soon, Washington was leading all the military forces in Virginia.

In 1758, Washington was elected to Virginia's House of Burgesses, an assembly of elected officials representing the colony's counties, and he resigned his military commission. He married Martha Dandridge Custis, a widow with two children and a substantial fortune, on January 6, 1759.

Washington eagerly stepped into the role of father to Martha's two children. Later, when his stepson, John, died in 1781, Washington and Martha raised two of John's children. Washington was always close to his step-granddaughter, and in 1796, he wrote her a letter about love and marriage that is still studied today.

Commander in Chief

With his position in the House of Burgesses, Washington became fully involved in local politics. He was very aware of the colonists' growing anger toward Britain. At first, Washington sided more with the Loyalists, who supported the British monarchy and did not want to be an independent nation. But his involvement in politics guided him to the belief the colonies must be free of British rule.

In 1774, he was elected as one of the Virginia delegates to the First Continental Congress, a special convention of representatives from the colonies called together in response to growing resistance to British rule. In 1775, the Second Continental Congress collectively nominated Washington as commander in chief of the Continental army, which would fight the British for independence in the American Revolution (1775–1783).

Washington's new role gave him command of an army that at times reached 20,000 men. In the course of the American Revolution, Washington won stunning victories, including forcing out the British during the Siege of Boston, which ended in March 1776. But he also experienced devastating

A CLOSER LOOK AT GEORGE WASHINGTON

Washington crosses the Delaware River, turning the tides of the war and changing his life forever.

defeats, such as losing 5,000 men at the Battle of Long Island in August 1776, when New York was lost to the British.

Washington rallied his forces. On Christmas night in 1776, in what would become a pivotal point of the war and his life, Washington led 2,400 men across the Delaware River to Trenton, New Jersey.

17

He took the enemy forces by surprise, defeating them in less than two hours.

In late September 1781, Washington laid siege to British troops in Yorktown, Virginia, with the help of the French army. The British surrendered, and the American Revolution soon came to an end. In 1783, after the Treaty of Paris was signed and the last of the British soldiers left New York, Washington resigned from his military career.

Becoming President

Washington was chosen as one of Virginia's seven delegates to the Constitutional Convention in Philadelphia, Pennsylvania, in May 1787. The convention met to draft a constitution for the newly formed nation of the United States of America. Thanks to Washington's support and his popularity with the delegates, the US Constitution was ratified in 1788. Washington had hoped to return to farming, but in early 1789, members of the Electoral College unanimously nominated him as the new nation's first president. On April 30, 1789, he accepted the oath of office, delivered the nation's first-ever inaugural address, and began his career as president.

In many ways, Washington designed the presidency, setting the example for all other presidents who followed. He also did much during his first term to benefit the new nation. He established a cabinet of advisors. He was the first to use the presidential veto. He established the first federal bank of the United States. He convinced the federal government to assume the states' debts from the war. And he spent a significant amount of time planning the new national capital, which now bears his name as Washington DC.

Washington's first term as president was to end in 1792. But his colleagues were reluctant to let go of his excellent leadership qualities and sound judgment. They urged him to stay on for another term. On February 13, 1793, Washington was elected president for the second time.

During this term, he pushed for the United States to establish neutrality in international conflicts as well as establish its own identity rather than rely on other nations. He addressed civil unrest by sending troops to squelch the Whiskey Rebellion in 1794, which was the first time the government suppressed an uprising of citizens resisting federal law. Washington's second term also saw the emergence of two opposing political parties, the Federalists and the Republicans.

As he neared the end of his second term, Washington grew tired. Attacks by political opponents and the burdens of the presidency were becoming overwhelming. He announced he would not run for a third term, which was allowed at the time. On September 19, 1796, he published his Farewell Address to the American people. In March 1797, he retired as president.

Later Life

Washington spent his last few years with his family at his beloved Mount Vernon. He renovated the home's interior and developed new techniques for planting wheat. In July 1799, Washington drafted his last will and testament. In his will, he included a provision to free his slaves after his and Martha's deaths, an act that still produces debate and interest today. Six months after drafting his will, Washington fell ill from riding in cold, wet weather. He died on December 14, 1799, at age 67.

Many Americans went into mourning. The country had lost a great military man and its first president. Citizens and government officials alike

A CLOSER LOOK AT GEORGE WASHINGTON

The nation's capital bears Washington's name, and the Washington Monument represents his greatness.

grieved the loss of Washington's strong leadership skills, solid advice, and overall decency. General Henry Lee, Washington's colleague, spoke for the nation, saying Washington was "first in war, first in peace, and first in the hearts of his countrymen."[1]

The first president of the United States takes the oath of office and delivers his inaugural address.

Chapter

3

An Overview of Washington's First Inaugural Address

Historical Context

On April 30, 1789, Washington was inaugurated as the first president of the newly founded United States. Much fanfare accompanied the formal ceremony. Soldiers, a band, and members of Congress escorted Washington to Federal Hall in New York City, then the nation's capital. There, the new president took the oath of office in front of 10,000 people. According to historian Jared Sparks, after the new president took his oath, "the air was rent by repeated shouts and huzzas,—'God bless our Washington! Long live our beloved President!'"[1]

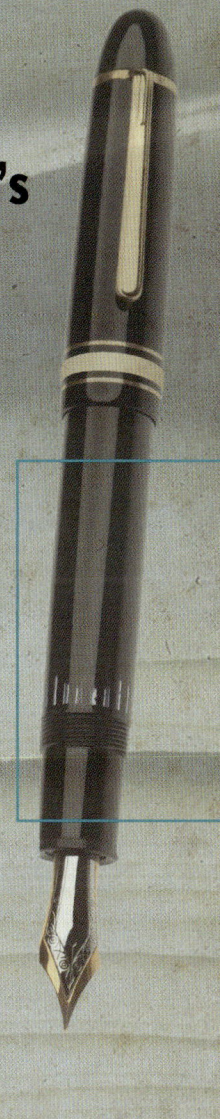

Although taking the oath was all Washington was required to do, he then delivered a speech to Congress. In this inaugural address, he rationalized his reluctance at accepting the presidency but also inspired to unite Americans in patriotism. Washington had taken a cautious approach to writing his address, working on it several months in advance. He asked several friends and colleagues to make suggestions to the speech, but he wrote the majority himself.

On the day of the inauguration, Washington read his address to the large crowd. Not comfortable with public speaking, however, his awkwardness was visible to the attendees. According to William Maclay, a senator from Pennsylvania, "This great man was agitated and embarrassed [by speaking] more than ever he was by the leveled cannon or pointed musket."[2] But the power of the president's words was also apparent. Fisher Ames, a representative from Massachusetts, said, "His aspect grave, almost to sadness; his modesty, actually shaking; his voice deep, a little tremulous, and so low as to call for close attention."[3]

A Closer Look at the First Inaugural Address

Washington's first inaugural address is written in a formal tone and divided into seven paragraphs. Washington begins by humbly revealing his insecurities, reluctance, and lack of confidence at accepting such an official position. Referring to the official notification of his nomination two weeks earlier, he says, "no event could have filled me with greater anxieties."[4] But he also contends the nomination is a call from the country he loves. He states he is uncertain he is qualified to execute the duties of the presidency. He admits it is a hardship to be taken from his enjoyable retirement. He also suggests he has inherited "inferior endowments from nature" and is "unpractised in the duties of civil administration."[5] But after taking all these factors into consideration, Washington accepts the position of president, trusting his fellow citizens will understand his motive is love for his country.

Washington goes on to hope the "Almighty Being who rules over the Universe" will bless the new US government with success.[6] He believes there has been a divine role in the formation of the nation.

Next, Washington offers his own understanding of the newly created role of president. He quotes the Constitution: "it is made the duty of the President 'to recommend to [Congress's] consideration, such measures as he shall judge necessary and expedient.'"[7] As head of the executive branch, he also trusts "no local prejudices, or attachments, no separate views, nor party animosities" will lead Congress astray in its legislative role.[8]

Washington affirms the new nation he has been called upon to lead will unite "virtue and happiness" and "duty and advantage."[9] He reminds Congressmen the "preservation of the sacred fire of liberty" and the "destiny of the Republican model of government" rests on their shoulders.[10] Washington references Article V of the Constitution, which gives Congress the right to propose amendments to the Constitution. He says he trusts Congress to decide when and how to best work under this article.

Washington stresses he has refused financial compensation for carrying out the duties of the presidency. He feels this is a selfless act of public service and should not be sullied with monetary gains. If he must receive compensation, he asks it "be limited to such actual expenditures as the public good may be thought to require."[11]

In his concluding paragraph, Washington once again calls upon "the benign parent of the human race."[12] He asks the divine power to bless the

AN OVERVIEW OF WASHINGTON'S FIRST INAUGURAL ADDRESS

new nation in creating an undivided, successful, and secure government that places its citizens' satisfaction and happiness as its main priority.

Washington reassures members of Congress he is confident in their abilities to govern the new nation.

As he assumes the new role of president, Washington hopes to gain credibility with his inaugural address.

Chapter 4

How to Apply Biographical Criticism to Washington's First Inaugural Address

What Is Biographical Criticism?

Biographical criticism analyzes how an author's life affects and inspires his or her works. In other words, understanding an author's life provides a better understanding of the author's works. Biographical criticism does not analyze a biography of the author's life, however. Instead, critics use biographical information to improve the reader's understanding, allowing the spotlight to remain on the original work.

Applying Biographical Criticism to Washington's First Inaugural Address

As Washington accepted the post of first president of the United States of America, he understood the full weight of responsibility being

How to Analyze the Works of GEORGE WASHINGTON

transferred to him. The newly independent nation had only recently liberated itself from British rule, and already the country was facing political issues, such as the divisiveness of states and political parties, civil unrest, and conflicts over slavery. Washington realized he was entrusted with the presidency because he had proven himself a successful military leader and a sensible delegate in the forging of the Constitution. In his first inaugural address, Washington emphasizes his reluctance to become president and downplays his qualifications in order to gain credibility, as these are the very qualities that will make him a strong and dedicated president.

Washington was anxious about becoming president because he did not know what to expect or what was expected of him. As a result, he was reluctant to assume the responsibilities

> **Thesis Statement**
> The thesis states, "In his first inaugural address, Washington emphasizes his reluctance to become president and downplays his qualifications in order to gain credibility, as these are the very qualities that will make him a strong and dedicated president." The essay shows how Washington highlights his humility in order to gain credibility as a strong leader.

> **Argument One**
> The author begins to support the thesis with the first argument: "Washington was anxious about becoming president because he did not know what to expect or what was expected of him." Here, the author discusses Washington's uncertainty at governing the nation because it is a new country and a new role.

of such a significant and influential role. In his inaugural address, Washington speaks of the "magnitude and difficulty" of the task bestowed on him by his country.[1] He states, "no event could have filled me with greater anxieties."[2] The sentiments in the address mirror sentiments in Washington's writings prior to the inauguration, such as when he expresses his feelings in his journal:

> *With a mind oppressed with more anxious and painful sensations than I have words to express, [I] set out for New York . . . to render service to my country in obedience to its call, but with less hope of answering its expectations.*[3]

Also, in a private letter to a friend before the inauguration, Washington writes,

> *I assure you . . . my movements to the chair of Government will be accompanied with feelings not unlike those of a culprit who is going to the place of his execution: so unwilling am I . . . to quit a peaceful abode for an Ocean of difficulties, without that competency of political skill—abilities & inclination which is necessary to manage the helm.*[4]

Washington is anxious because he knows the task he is about to undertake is monumental and has never been undertaken before: becoming the president of this new democracy.

<u>As he humbly accepts the duty of the presidency, Washington acknowledges his perceived academic shortcomings and lack of traditional political training.</u> Because of his father's death and his meager inheritance, Washington could not go abroad for his formal education as was the norm among the American aristocracy. Throughout his life, Washington was sensitive about his lack of formal education. One of his first statements in the inaugural address expresses this humility:

> The magnitude and difficulty of the trust to which the voice of my Country called me . . . could not but overwhelm with despondence, one, who, inheriting inferior endowments from nature and unpractised in the duties of

Argument Two
The author continues to support the thesis by stating, "As he humbly accepts the duty of the presidency, Washington acknowledges his perceived academic shortcomings and lack of traditional political training." In this paragraph, the author focuses on Washington's lack of formal education and how he compensated for it by other means.

civil administration, ought to be peculiarly conscious of his own deficiencies.[5]

Despite his insecurities about his education, Washington clearly expanded his knowledge and proved himself as a prominent leader through his own merits. He made strong political and social connections, which allowed him to strengthen his character and gain leadership skills. This led him to his military career that ultimately launched him into the nation's spotlight. As he delivers his inaugural address, Washington is aware of his academic shortcomings, but he is also aware of his upstanding qualities. By humbly downplaying his qualifications in his address, he presents himself as a self-made man of good character—with fine qualities for serving as president.

<u>Washington stresses he does not accept the presidency as a way to gain status or wealth, creating the impression he will be a dedicated, selfless president.</u> Washington did not actively seek the presidency; rather, his peers and colleagues unanimously elected him to it.

Argument Three
The author goes on to argue, "Washington stresses he does not accept the presidency as a way to gain status or wealth, creating the impression he will be a dedicated, selfless president." This argument discusses Washington's lack of ulterior motives for running the nation.

How to Analyze the Works of **GEORGE WASHINGTON**

Although he is loved by many Americans, Washington stresses he does not seek fame, fortune, or power with the presidency.

In his address, Washington describes how he came to accept the nomination: "I was summoned by my Country, whose voice I can never hear but with veneration and love."[6] In addition, Washington declares financial gain is not part of his agenda, as he requests any compensation "be limited to such actual expenditures as the public good may be thought to require."[7] While it is true Washington entered the presidency already an independently wealthy and celebrated man, focusing on his selfless motives still emphasizes his integrity to his

HOW TO APPLY BIOGRAPHICAL CRITICISM TO WASHINGTON'S FIRST INAUGURAL ADDRESS

audience and builds credibility with them.

<u>Washington also emphasizes he is not seeking unlimited political power as president.</u> After leading the United States' struggle to gain independence from a monarchy, Washington understood people's anxiety about choosing a single leader to run the new nation. In his address, Washington emphasizes the authority as well as the limits of his role as president. Quoting the Constitution, he states, "By the article establishing the Executive Department, it is made the duty of the President 'to recommend to your consideration, such measures as he shall judge necessary and expedient.'"[8] Washington acknowledges the Constitution establishes the president as the leader of the executive branch, yet he asserts he will not encroach on Congress's authority in the legislative branch. In a sign of respect, he compliments "the talents, the rectitude, and the patriotism" of the Congressmen and places his full trust in their ability to govern wisely.[9] By acknowledging the limitations

> **Argument Four**
> The fourth argument states: "Washington also emphasizes he is not seeking unlimited political power as president." This paragraph addresses how Washington acknowledges the authority and the limits of his power as president.

of his power as president and showing respect to Congress, Washington builds the credibility he needs in order to lead the new nation.

> **Conclusion**
> The conclusion sums up the author's thesis and arguments. It also provides a new idea: as Washington emphasizes his shortcomings and selfless motives, he sets an example for future presidents.

Aware of the challenge ahead of him, his shortcomings, and the nation's desire for a president of good character, Washington stresses his reluctance in his first inaugural address. But at the same time, he displays the humble, honest, and trustworthy qualities that will no doubt make him a strong president. His humble reluctance set the tone for future presidents to invoke selfless dedication and an honest moral ethic for the leadership of the United States of America.

Thinking Critically about Washington's First Inaugural Address

Now it is your turn to assess the critique. Consider these questions:

1. Which argument do you think is the strongest? Which is the weakest?

2. In the first argument, the author quotes two other sources in which Washington speaks of his reluctance to become president. Do these quotes help strengthen the argument? Why or why not?

3. The author argues Washington emphasizes his reluctance and lack of qualifications in order to show how they will make him a strong president. Do you agree? Does other evidence from the speech support this argument?

Other Approaches

Biographical criticism analyzes how an author's works are inspired by his or her life. Knowing the background of the writer's life allows the reader to delve deeper into the author's projected meaning. One way to apply biographical criticism to Washington's first inaugural address is illustrated in the essay above. Two alternate approaches are discussed below. The first approach focuses on Washington's refusal of financial compensation as president. The second approach considers how losing his father early in life affected Washington's education and future.

An Unpaid President

Washington refused monetary reimbursement for his official service to the people of the United States of America. Washington writes, "When I was first honored with a call into the service of my country . . . the light in which I contemplated my duty required that I should renounce every pecuniary compensation."[10] This statement reflects Washington's goal to present himself as a dedicated president not motivated by financial or other selfish rewards. A possible thesis statement based on this point could be: Washington set an example for future presidents by saying their position should be selflessly dedicated to serving the public above financial interests.

The Importance of Not Being Educated

Receiving only a small inheritance upon his father's death, Washington could not pursue a formal education in Britain as did many of his contemporaries. Although Washington presents this as a flaw in his inaugural address, one can argue it is actually a benefit. Free from British connections and influence, he can stress his dedication to the United States and his ability and desire to lead it through its new independence. A possible thesis statement addressing this biographical factor could be: Being denied a formal British education allowed Washington to develop the personal philosophy and characteristics necessary to become the first president of the United States.

When his step-granddaughter Nelly says she is not interested in romance, Washington pens her some advice.

Chapter 5

An Overview of "Washington's Advice on Love & Marriage"

Historical Context

In 1758, Washington married a young widow named Martha Custis with two children, John and Patsy, from her previous marriage. Washington had no children of his own with Martha, but he was very loving toward his stepchildren. However, Patsy died at age 17 due to medical complications, and John died of fever at age 27 while serving as an aide to Washington during the American Revolution.

After John's death, Washington and Martha took in two of his four children, Eleanor "Nelly" Custis and George "Washy" Custis. Martha and Washington were very devoted and raised their two grandchildren with much affection. Nelly quickly became Washington's favorite. He especially relished her bright, lively personality.

Source of Advice

Washington's relations often came to him, the father figure, for advice. On March 21, 1796, Washington penned a letter to Nelly regarding the subject of love and passion. Nelly had written a previous letter to Washington, revealing she did not think she would ever marry, for she took no interest in the young men who attempted to court her. Washington's reply to Nelly was originally included as "Washington's Advice on Love & Marriage" in the 1861 book *Recollections of Washington*, compiled by Nelly's brother George.

Washington's advice may reflect his own experiences. Historians believe that before meeting Martha, Washington had fallen in love with a married woman named Sally Fairfax. He knew he could not act on this love, however, and his passion for Fairfax eventually faded. By many accounts, Washington and Martha enjoyed a loving marriage, though perhaps one based on friendship more than on passion.

Love Letters

Washington begins the letter by alluding to a promise he had made to write to Nelly every time she wrote to him. He says although he has indeed given her "letter for letter," he has delayed too long in doing so.[1] Washington goes on to compliment Nelly's manner of writing, noting her "ideas are lively" and her "descriptions agreeable."[2] He admonishes her, though, scolding that her previous letters to her grandmother "appear to have been written in too much haste."[3]

Washington dedicates the rest of the letter to advice on romance and marriage. Washington addresses Nelly's previous declaration that she had no interest in the "youth of the present day" and was determined "*never* to give herself a moment's uneasiness on account of them."[4] He gives her a hint: the feelings between men and women have remained unchanged over the course of time and she too may one day find she has fallen in love. He states about love, "Do not therefore boast too soon, nor too strongly, of your insensibility to, or resistance of its powers."[5] He suggests she may someday meet a man who fires her own passion. For this reason, his letter will serve as a lecture, or advice, about love.

Washington acknowledges that love "is said to be an involuntary passion"—one a person cannot resist.[6] While he agrees this is true to some extent, he contends passion can be "stifled" or "stunted" if a person is kept from the object of passion.[7] He uses the example of a woman who draws the attention of many men. Once she is married, the other men lose their feelings for her because they have no hope of attaining her. Because love is not involuntary, Washington argues it "ought to be under the guidance of reason."[8] He advises Nelly to follow her plan to "love with moderation," adding, "at least until you have secured your game."[9] By this he means until she knows the proper way to conduct herself in matters of love.

Washington goes on to give specific instructions about this conduct. He tells Nelly she should look for particular qualities in a husband. For example: Can the man provide for her financially? Is he a man of good character and good sense? Washington claims, "a sensible woman can never be happy with a fool."[10] And finally, is she sure about his "affections" toward her—or is she harboring feelings not reciprocated by the man?[11]

Washington stresses the man must first declare his feelings—"without the most indirect invitation" from her—in order for their love to be valid and

AN OVERVIEW OF "WASHINGTON'S ADVICE ON LOVE & MARRIAGE"

George and Martha Washington, depicted here at their wedding, seemed to enjoy a good marriage.

proper.[12] He warns her not to be prudish, or overly modest, but also not to be coquettish, or insincerely flirtatious. As he explains, women of either behavior often end up alone because their actions are improper and "punished" by sensible men.[13]

Washington ends the letter by celebrating Nelly's sister's recent marriage, suggesting the marriage fulfills the sister's "fondest desires" and hoping it brings her "future happiness."[14] Turning his focus back to Nelly, he leaves her with a final wish, that "every blessing, among which a good husband when you want & deserve one, is bestowed on you."[15] Three years later, Nelly would marry Washington's nephew Lawrence Lewis.

45

Washington's advice to Nelly reveals much about the roles women were expected to play in 1796.

Chapter

6

How to Apply Feminist Criticism to "Washington's Advice on Love & Marriage"

What Is Feminist Criticism?

Feminist criticism addresses the roles of women in works written by both men and women. When analyzing a work from a feminist perspective, a critic might examine how women are characterized or addressed, especially within the context of a male-dominated culture. Does a work portray women as marginalized? Does it elevate men in dominant positions? Such questions can help a critic determine whether a work upholds or challenges common gender roles.

Applying Feminist Criticism to "Washington's Advice on Love & Marriage"

Washington belonged to a male-dominated culture of the eighteenth century. Women were

How to Analyze the Works of **GEORGE WASHINGTON**

marginalized in most social dynamics, including love and marriage. When his step-granddaughter Nelly claims she has little interest in romance and is "resistant of its powers," Washington replies with a letter full of advice.[1] While advising Nelly, Washington upholds eighteenth-century gender roles in which women have little power, even in matters of love.

Washington instructs Nelly to consider how well a future husband can support her, implying women are dependent upon men. If Nelly should find her "heart growing warm," Washington directs her to ask the following questions:[2]

> Is he a man of good character? A man of sense? For be assured a sensible woman can never be happy with a fool. What has been his walk in life? Is he a gambler? a spendthrift,

---

Thesis Statement

The thesis states, "While advising Nelly, Washington upholds eighteenth-century gender roles in which women have little power, even in matters of love." The author supports this argument by discussing the gender roles Washington's letter reflects and supports.

Argument One

The author begins arguing the thesis by stating, "Washington instructs Nelly to consider how well a future husband can support her, implying women are dependent upon men." The author supports this argument by discussing the questions Washington instructs Nelly to ask herself about a future husband.

a drunkard? Is his fortune sufficient to maintain me in the manner I have been accustomed to live, and my sisters do live?[3]

Following these questions would lead women like Nelly to choose husbands who are upstanding men capable of providing for their wives and families. He warns against gamblers and others who may be financially unreliable. Washington's advice upholds the gender roles of the time in which women rely upon their husbands for financial support. In other words, women must choose their husbands from a position of dependency. It also suggests women are powerless to support themselves or change their husbands' behaviors if the men are financially irresponsible.

<u>Washington also advises Nelly about attracting men with the proper level of physical charm, upholding the gender role that women must match men's expectations to gain their affections.</u> Washington gives an example of how a man turns to "madness" for the "charms" of

> **Argument Two**
> The second argument states, "Washington also advises Nelly about attracting men with the proper level of physical charm, upholding the gender role that women must match men's expectations to gain their affections." The author analyzes how Washington's advice suggests men have almost impossible requirements for women's behavior.

How to Analyze the Works of **GEORGE WASHINGTON**

a woman "all beautiful & accomplished."[4] But it seems men demand an impossibly exact amount of charm, as Washington warns Nelly to be neither prudish nor coquettish. According to Washington,

> Nothing short of good sense, and an easy unaffected conduct can draw the line between prudery & coquetry; both of which are equally despised by men of understanding; and soon or late, will recoil upon the actor.[5]

Washington harshly states a "coquette dies in celibacy, as a punishment for her attempts [to]

Even this scene of Washington first meeting Martha shows the gender roles men and women assume in matters of romance.

50

HOW TO APPLY FEMINIST CRITICISM TO "WASHINGTON'S ADVICE ON LOVE & MARRIAGE"

mislead others . . . for no other purpose than to draw men on . . . that they may be rejected."[6] Men, it seems, are willing to fall into madness over charming women, but they will punish women who use those charms to make fools of them. On the other hand, being prudish is "equally despised," as men demand a certain amount of "blaze."[7] Again, Washington notes both prudery and coquetry will be "punished by the counter game of men."[8] The clear implication is that women must meet men's expectations for physical charm or they will be punished.

<u>Washington's recommendations to Nelly further imply men control affectionate relationships, whereas women must play a submissive role.</u> According to Washington, Nelly must not make any advances toward a man. She must instead wait for him to declare himself to her:

> Delicacy, custom, or call it by what epithet you will having precluded all advances on your part, the declaration without the most

---

Argument Three

The third argument states: "Washington's recommendations to Nelly further imply men control affectionate relationships, whereas women must play a submissive role." This argument discusses how women must play a passive role in relationships.

indirect invitation on yours *must proceed from the* man *to render it permanent & valuable.*[9]

The message is clear that women must refrain from making even indirect advances toward men. Instead, they must be submissive recipients of men's declarations. In fact, a woman's own affections will not be "valuable" or "permanent" if she takes an assertive role.[10] The dynamics leave women with little to no power.

Washington's letter to Nelly encourages her to seek a financially supportive husband, meet men's expectations about charm, and allow the man to take the lead in a relationship. This advice reinforces the gender roles of the male-dominated, eighteenth-century American culture. One must wonder, perhaps, whether Nelly was truly resisting the powers of love, or whether she was resisting the submissive role she was required to play.

> **Conclusion**
> This final paragraph is the conclusion of the critique. It sums up the author's arguments and partially restates the original thesis. The conclusion also provides the reader with a new idea: perhaps Nelly resisted the gender role required of women in romantic relationships.

Thinking Critically about "Washington's Advice on Love & Marriage"

Now it is your turn to assess the critique. Consider these questions:

1. The author argues Washington's letter to Nelly reflects eighteenth-century gender roles. Do you agree with this argument? Why or why not?

2. Which argument makes the strongest point? Which would benefit from more support?

3. The conclusion should restate the thesis and arguments discussed in the essay. Does the conclusion do this effectively? Why or why not?

Other Approaches

Feminist criticism generally focuses on gender inequality, examining the balance between the role of males and females in a piece of writing. One possible way to apply feminist criticism to "Washington's Advice on Love & Marriage" is shown in the essay above. A different approach might consider Washington's ideas regarding how women are powerless against their own passions. Another approach could focus on Washington's view of his step-granddaughter as a strong and independent woman.

A Woman's Passion

In his letter, Washington assumes Nelly will one day want a husband, despite her assertion none of the young men she encountered interested her. He implies because she is a woman, her passions will be easily enflamed, even if she wishes to remain single. Of women, he states, "the passions of your sex are easier roused than allayed."[11] A thesis addressing this topic might read: Because Nelly is a woman, Washington assumes she has no power to stop her own passion.

Strong Women

"Washington's Advice on Love & Marriage" reveals he views Nelly as a strong, smart woman. He compliments her writing and encourages her to seek a "man of sense," since "a sensible woman can never be happy with a fool."[12] But because she is strong, perhaps Washington feels the need to mold her into the proper role in order for her to find a husband. A thesis focusing on this topic might be: Because Washington regards Nelly as an intelligent and independent young woman, he feels she needs special instruction about the submissive role she must assume in matters of love.

Instead of delivering his Farewell Address as a speech, Washington published it in newspapers in September 1796.

Chapter 7

An Overview of Washington's Farewell Address

Historical Context

Toward the end of his second term as president, Washington felt the burdens of the presidency were overwhelming. In September 1796, he decided not to run for a third term, which caused a public outcry. In response, he composed his Farewell Address as a legacy and as a guide for future presidents and the nation. He enlisted Alexander Hamilton, his secretary of the treasury and closest adviser, and James Madison, known as the Father of the Constitution, to help him write his address. It would sum up and defend his administration. It would also serve as a warning about the potential hazards threatening the young nation.

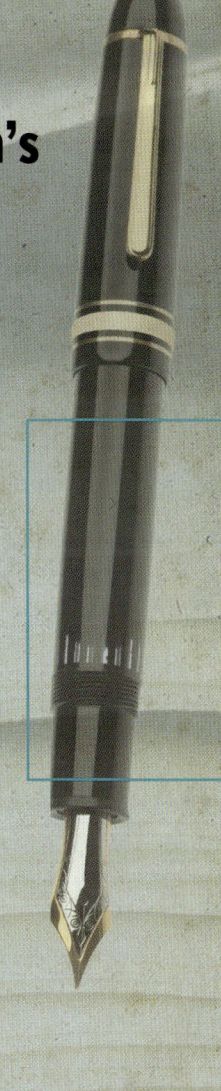

Washington did not deliver his Farewell Address as a speech; rather, he chose to have it published in a newspaper. The Farewell Address was first published in the *American Daily Advertiser* on September 19, 1796. Other newspapers picked up the address soon afterward and printed it throughout the country.

A Farewell to the Country

Washington begins his Farewell Address by informing the nation he will not include his name on the list of candidates as the new presidential election approaches. He asserts this reflects "no diminution of zeal for your future interest, no deficiency of grateful respect for your past kindness."[1] Instead, he says, he is now taking the opportunity to "return to that retirement from which I had been reluctantly drawn."[2] He admits he had initially composed an address to conclude his first term as president, not expecting to serve a second term. But the country's "critical posture of . . . affairs with foreign nations" caused him to abandon his original plans and begin the second term in 1793. Now, however, he feels the country is in better standing to allow him to retire.

Washington declares he has tried to fulfill his position well, but even after eight years, he still does not feel confident in his own abilities.

In addition, he notices the effects of aging and feels it is necessary to retire. Before he leaves public life, however, he wants to acknowledge his gratitude to his "beloved country for the many honors it has conferred upon me; still more for the steadfast confidence with which it has supported me."[3] If anything good has come from his presidency, Washington credits it to the American people for their constant support. He hopes now the country's "union and brotherly affection may be perpetual; that the free constitution . . . may be sacredly maintained."[4]

A United Nation

To this end, Washington offers advice out of love for the nation. He stresses unity, stating,

> *[It is the] main pillar in the edifice of your real independence, the support of your tranquility at home, your peace abroad; of your safety; of your prosperity; of that very Liberty, which you so highly prize.*[5]

Washington reminds Americans they are all "citizens, by birth or choice, of a common country."[6] Thus, they must always take pride in "the name of American."[7]

Washington then warns about forces seeking to undermine the nation's unity. One such force is the perceived division between different regions of the country. Washington addresses divisions between the North, with its manufacturing, and the South, with its agriculture. Washington claims the separate areas of the country need one another: "All the parts combined cannot fail to find . . . greater strength, greater resource . . . greater security from external danger."[8] By remaining united, the states can avoid civil wars. He also emphasizes how all citizens from each region must respect the federal government and obey its laws: "Respect for its authority, compliance with its laws, acquiescence in its measures, are duties enjoined by the fundamental maxims of true Liberty."[9]

Political Parties and Power

Washington advises the nation against the political party system, another force dividing the country. A divided government is a weak government, he says. Political parties play regional and ideological differences to their own advantages—but to the nation's disadvantage. In addition, parties try to dominate one another with a spirit of revenge. He warns this disorder could eventually lead citizens to seek stability in "the absolute power of an individual" ruler.[10] Such an event would be the "ruins of Public Liberty," which Americans had so recently fought to win.[11]

Even as he encourages the nation to remain united, Washington warns against letting any single part of the government become too powerful. He recognizes how a "love of power, and the proneness to abuse it . . . predominates in the human heart."[12] Such abuses must be prevented. If governmental powers must be shifted, he argues, such a shift should be carried out with an amendment to the Constitution, not by force.

Washington states one way to strengthen the nation is to use public credit, although sparingly. If debt is accrued, it should be paid back in a timely manner to avoid "ungenerously throwing upon posterity the [burden], which we ourselves ought to bear."[13] Washington reminds citizens the country needs revenue to pay debt. And in order to have revenue, "there must be taxes," even though they are "more or less inconvenient and unpleasant."[14]

Foreign Affairs

Next, Washington discusses foreign influence. He encourages the young nation to "observe good faith and justice towards all Nations."[15] The country should neither hate any nation nor hold any as a favorite. Otherwise, it will be a "slave" to those nations, and there will be risks of war.[16] Washington advises, "It is our true policy to steer clear of permanent alliances with any portion of the foreign world."[17] After all, he states, European interests have little to do with the new nation.

Concluding Words

Washington concludes by saying he fears his advice will not "make the strong and lasting impression I could wish."[18] But he does hope this advice will serve some good, because these same ideas have served him well as president. Yet, he admits his presidency has not been without mistakes:

> *Though, in reviewing the incidents of my administration, I am unconscious of intentional error, I am nevertheless too sensible of my defects not to think it*

AN OVERVIEW OF WASHINGTON'S FAREWELL ADDRESS

probable that I may have committed many errors.[19]

Finally, Washington looks forward to enjoying the benefit of "good laws under a free government," now that he is an ordinary citizen of his country.[20]

Washington looked forward to retirement at his beloved Mount Vernon home.

Essential Critiques

How to Analyze the Works of GEORGE WASHINGTON

As his presidency comes to an end, Washington is concerned about the fragile unity of the new nation.

Chapter 8

How to Apply Historical Criticism to Washington's Farewell Address

What Is Historical Criticism?

Historical criticism analyzes a work from the perspective of the social, political, and economic circumstances of the time it was created. An effective historical critique, then, focuses on the impact of cultural trends and historical events on the work. Historical critics analyze the text itself, but they also consider how cultural and historical events affect that text. According to critics, awareness of the historical background can shed new light on a literary work.

Applying Historical Criticism to Washington's Farewell Address

Soon after the United States gained its freedom from Britain, forces both inside and outside of

How to Analyze the Works of **GEORGE WASHINGTON**

> **Thesis Statement**
> The thesis states: "Washington's Farewell Address warns of the factors inside and outside the nation that threatened democracy, liberty, and the nation as a whole at that point in history." This thesis proposes his Farewell Address discusses the threats to national unity and preservation he has observed during his time as president.

> **Argument One**
> The author presents the first argument in support of the thesis: "Washington's address hopes to discourage Americans from thinking of themselves as separate regions rather than united parts of one nation."
> The argument details the regionalism affecting the nation.

the country began to create problems. As the first president, Washington was concerned about these forces, especially as he announced in 1796 that he would not seek a third term. **Washington's Farewell Address warns of the factors inside and outside the nation that threatened democracy, liberty, and the nation as a whole at that point in history.**

<u>Washington's address hopes to discourage Americans from thinking of themselves as separate regions rather than united parts of one nation.</u> Washington was elected president shortly after the colonies became a nation. Now he seeks to unite the disparate states as a country: "The name of American, which belongs to you, in your national capacity, must always exalt the just pride of Patriotism, more than any appellation derived from local

discriminations."[1] Many citizens still did not think of themselves as belonging to one nation, which led to conflicts and weakened the nation. In his address, Washington stresses unity, as "all the parts combined cannot fail to find in the united mass of means and efforts greater strength."[2] Taking the idea one step further, Washington upholds the authority of the federal government as the unifying power: "To the efficacy and permanency of your Union, a Government for the whole is indispensable. No alliances, however strict, between the parts can be an adequate substitute."[3]

<u>Also aware of the party divisions threatening the country, Washington warns unrestrained political dissension puts liberty at risk.</u> By the end of Washington's second term, the national government had split into two distinct and oppositional political parties: the Federalists, led by Alexander Hamilton, and the Republicans, led by Thomas Jefferson. In his address, Washington acknowledges "there is an opinion, that parties in free countries

> **Argument Two**
> The author continues to support the thesis with the second argument: "Also aware of the party divisions threatening the country, Washington warns unrestrained political dissension puts liberty at risk." In this argument, the author addresses Washington's concerns about oppositional political parties.

How to Analyze the Works of **GEORGE WASHINGTON**

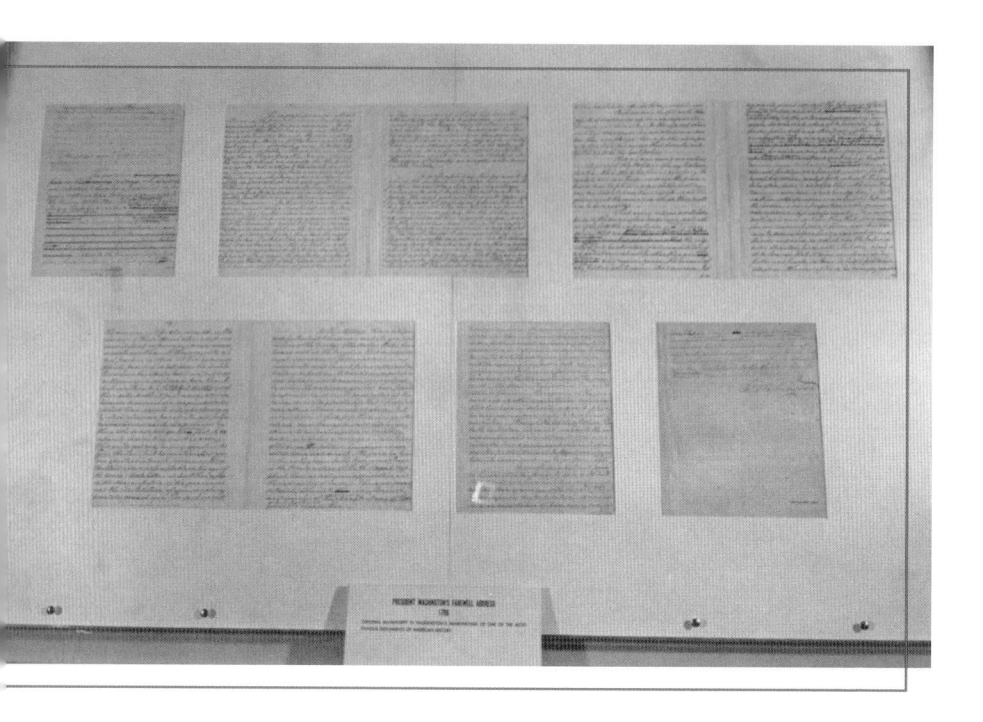

An original handwritten copy of Washington's Farewell Address on display

are useful checks upon the administration of the Government, and serve to keep alive the spirit of Liberty."[4] But he ultimately disagrees with unrestrained party division, stating it "kindles the animosity of one part against another."[5] He claims party division can lead to despotism, which is tyranny under an absolute leader:

> The alternate domination of one faction over another, sharpened by the spirit of revenge, natural to party dissension . . . is itself a frightful despotism. . . . The disorders and miseries, which result [from party division],

> *gradually incline the minds of men to seek security and repose in the absolute power of an individual.*[6]

That is, Washington cautions that political parties vying for power put democracy and liberty at risk.

Washington's address also focuses on threats outside the borders. <u>Having newly attained independence from Britain, Washington warns how emotional attachments to other nations put the United States at risk</u>. The goal, he contends, is to "observe good faith and justice towards all Nations; cultivate peace and harmony with all."[7] Washington stresses the United States should avoid strong animosity as well as strong favoritism toward other countries. He asserts,

> **Argument Three**
> The final argument states: "Having newly attained independence from Britain, Washington warns how emotional attachments to other nations put the United States at risk." The author analyzes Washington's opinion that emotional involvement with foreign nations endangers the United States.

> *The Nation, which indulges towards another an habitual hatred, or an habitual fondness, is in some degree a slave. It is a slave to its animosity or to its affection, either of which is sufficient to lead it astray from its duty and its interest.*[8]

Washington says strong foreign attachments can lead to unnecessary war and "the peace often, sometimes perhaps the liberty, of Nations has been the victim."[9] With the United States having recently waged war to gain its independence, Washington and his audience all recognize the need to protect the nation from such a threat.

Washington's Farewell Address reveals the factors that threatened the future of the United States at the time he stepped down from the presidency in 1796. He acknowledges the social and political divisions as well as the foreign attachments putting the nation at risk. But Washington's warnings are still applicable today. In fact, his Farewell Address is read each year by the US Senate. One can perhaps argue that although many things have changed since 1796, these same factors still pose a risk to the nation.

> **Conclusion**
> This final paragraph is the conclusion of the critique. It sums up the author's arguments and partially restates the thesis. The conclusion also provides a new idea: perhaps Washington's warnings are still applicable in US politics today.

Thinking Critically about Washington's Farewell Address

Now it is your turn to assess the critique. Consider these questions:

1. Do all of the author's arguments make strong points? Which need more support?

2. Could the author have included any additional arguments to show how Washington's address reflects the political concerns of the time?

3. Does the conclusion fit this essay well? Do you agree Washington's warnings still apply today?

Other Approaches

Historical criticism examines how a work is influenced by the social, political, and economic circumstances of its time. One possible way to apply historical literary criticism to Washington's Farewell Address is highlighted in the essay above. Two alternate approaches are discussed below. The first approach addresses Washington's emphasis on American patriotism. The second approach focuses on the value Washington placed on religion and ethical morality in politics.

National Identity

To many citizens and politicians of the time, the United States was just that—individual states loosely united. Many clung to their regional identities. In his Farewell Address, however, Washington uses persuasive arguments and his political stature to more firmly unite the states under one common nationality. He declares, "Citizens, by birth or choice, of a common country, that country has a right to concentrate your affections."[10] A possible thesis based on this idea could be: Washington attempts to unify the citizens of the United States by emphasizing their common identity as Americans.

An Ethical Politician

In the Constitution, specifically the First Amendment, the founding fathers addressed religion in light of government. The phrase "separation of church and state" is often used to describe the interpretation. But in his Farewell Address, Washington—an influential member of the Constitutional Convention—acknowledges the roles morality, spirituality, and ethics plays in the governing of the nation. He asserts, "Of all the dispositions and habits, which lead to political prosperity, Religion and Morality are indispensable supports."[11] A possible thesis related to this idea could be: Washington intends to create a code of ethics in his Farewell Address that encourages future politicians to use religion and morality as guides.

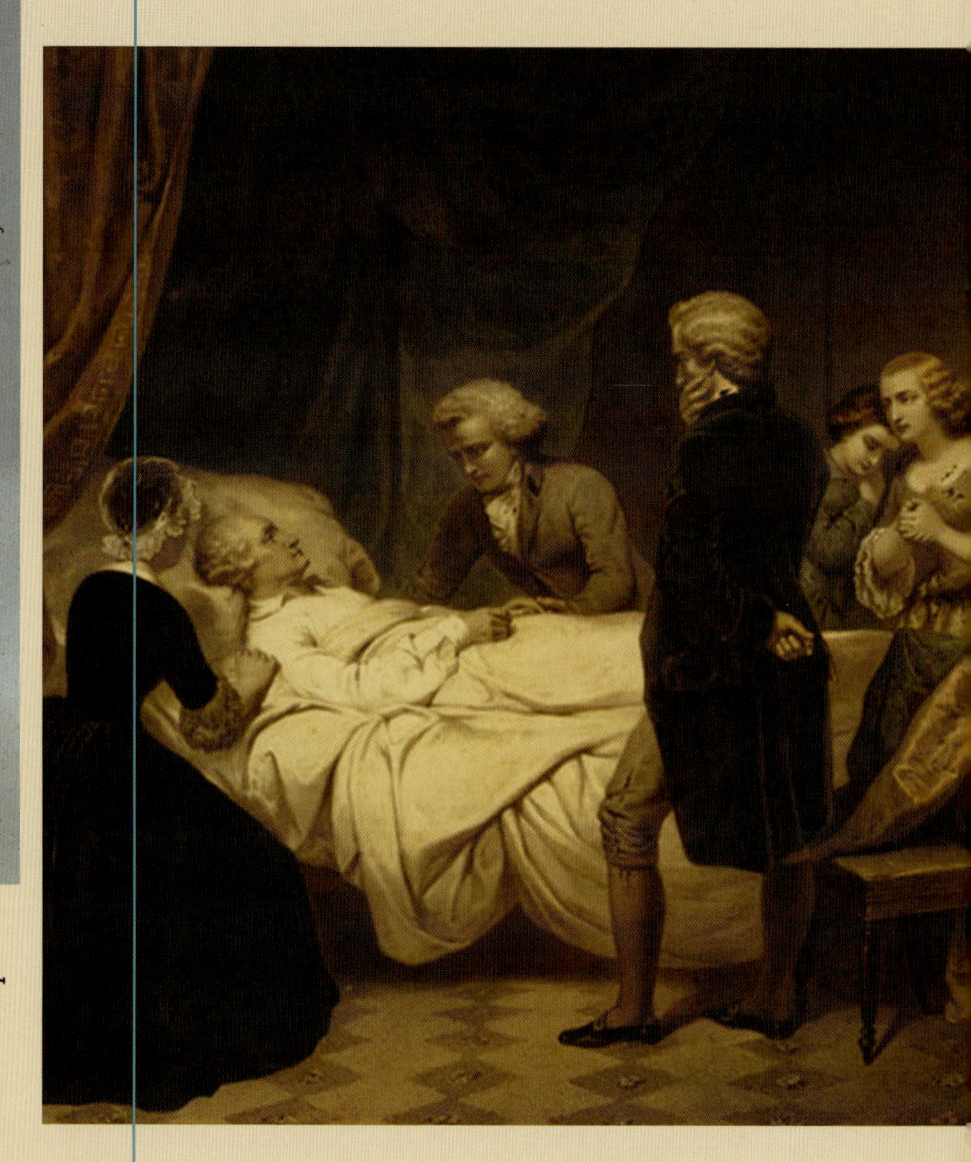

Six months before his death in December 1799, Washington signed his last will and testament.

Chapter 9

An Overview of Washington's Will

Historical Context

Having composed many important speeches and documents throughout his public and private life, George Washington composed a final document, his will, on July 9, 1799. The 29-page will gave detailed instructions regarding his estate after his death. It replaced a will he had written in 1775, shortly after being named president. One of the reasons Washington's will is considered such a historically important document is because of its explicit instructions for freeing the slaves he owned.

Washington and Slavery

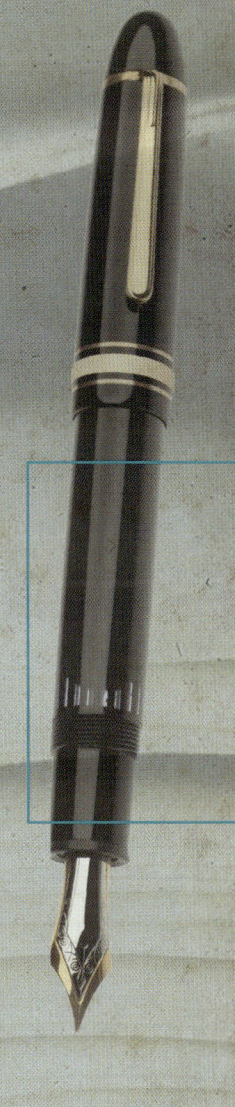

Washington lived in eighteenth-century Virginia, where many white people owned plantations and slaves. He became a slave owner at age 11, inheriting ten slaves after his father's death. Over the years, Washington also purchased a number of slaves of his own, many of them young women who would bear children and provide him with more slaves. (A baby born to a slave mother automatically became a slave as well.) Washington owned 124 slaves at the time he wrote his will. Martha owned 153 slaves as part of her dower from her first marriage to Daniel Parke Custis. These Custis slaves were not legally Washington's property, although he had use of them at Mount Vernon.

Last Will and Testament

Washington begins his will by providing for the payment of the few small debts outstanding at the time of his death. Then he makes sure Martha will be well cared for during her lifetime, leaving her the use and benefit of his entire estate and all its possessions. This was an uncommon practice at the time, when most husbands left their wives only a "widow's share," with the bulk of the estate going to the heirs.

Perhaps most notably, Washington's will directs that after Martha's death, all the slaves he owns are to be set free. He wishes he could free them immediately upon his death, but he wants to avoid splitting families. Many of his slaves have married the Custis slaves, whom Washington has no right or ability to set free. Thus, in order to avoid separating his slaves from their families, he sets the time of their emancipation after Martha's death. Some historians believe Washington had hoped Martha and her heirs would follow his example and free the Custis slaves as well, but this did not happen.

Not only does Washington grant his slaves freedom after Martha's death, but he also ensures those who are too old, too young, or too sick to support themselves will be fed and clothed by his heirs. Orphans are to remain with their masters or mistresses until they are 25 years old, and they are to be provided an education so they can eventually support themselves as free people. The old and infirm are to be provided proper medical care and housing. Moreover, Washington expressly forbids his family from selling any of his slaves before their emancipation, in case they may attempt to circumnavigate his wishes. He stresses the clause granting his slaves' freedom is to be explicitly followed.

How to Analyze the Works of GEORGE WASHINGTON

Martha too owned many slaves at Mount Vernon as part of her dower from her first husband's death.

Washington makes special provisions for his personal servant, a slave named William Lee. William may choose whether to go free immediately or remain in his current position. In either case, he is to receive an annual payment. Washington says he grants this to William "as a testimony of my sense of his attachment to me, and for his faithful service during the Revolutionary War."[1]

Education for Americans

In another clause of the will, Washington lists the shares, or stock, he has received as gifts from various companies over the years. Washington points out he had asked "not to receive pecuniary compensation for any services I could render my country in its arduous struggle with great Britain, for its Rights."[2] Yet, he says, he agreed to accept these shares with the understanding he would appoint the funds for public, rather than personal, use.

Washington now describes how these funds are to help establish a university. Washington laments the custom of young Americans leaving the country to continue their education. He fears foreign education teaches young people "principles unfriendly to Republican Government and to the true & genuine liberties of Mankind."[3] He donates a portion of the public-use funds to the District of Columbia to build a university where these young people can obtain a strong classical education in the United States. He hopes such an institution will allow students from across the country to form friendships free of "local prejudices" and help them understand they are part of a united nation.[4] This donation led to the creation of what is now George Washington University.

In addition to setting aside funds for a university, Washington also specifies how other funds are to be used for the education of American children. He sets aside $4,000 to establish a school in Alexandria, Virginia, committed to educating poor and orphaned children.

Freeing More Slaves

Next, Washington clears the debts of family members who owe him money. Most notably, he forgives the debt owed to him by Martha's deceased brother, Bartholomew Dandridge, and his heirs. In partial payment of this debt, the Dandridge family had given Washington 33 slaves, which he then leased back to Mary, Dandridge's widow. These slaves are his legal property, though not in his possession at Mount Vernon. In his will, he grants freedom to these slaves, although with special stipulations based on their ages. Older slaves are to be freed immediately, but younger slaves must provide many years of service to Dandridge's widow and heirs before they will be free.

Personal Bequests

Washington uses the remainder of his will to make a number of personal bequests. He leaves much of his estate at Mount Vernon, including his mansion house, to his nephew Bushrod Washington. He also leaves Bushrod the records of his civil and military service as well as his books. The rest of his estate at Mount Vernon he leaves to his step-granddaughter Nelly and her husband, since he considers "the Grand children of my wife in the same light as I do my own relations." Other land holdings are distributed to family members.

Washington divides his personal effects and furniture among his relatives and friends. Any items not expressly named in the will are to be sold, with the proceeds divided. Washington also advises the executors to not rush into selling his land, since property values are rising.

Final Wishes

As he concludes his will, Washington requests a new burial vault at Mount Vernon, in which his remains, as well as those of his family, may be placed. He desires his burial to be a private affair, "without parade, or funeral Oration."[6]

In its final words, Washington states that although the writing of his will "has occupied many of [his] leisure hours," he fears it will "appear crude and incorrect."[7] He has tried to state his wishes plainly, so no disputes will arise from the division of his property. If arguments do arise, Washington orders the parties to present their cases to three impartial men, who will make a final ruling.

Washington signs his will on July 9, 1799—which is, as he notes, the twenty-fourth year of the United States' independence. He died six months later on December 14, after falling ill in bad weather.

The Fate of the Slaves

Shortly after Washington's death, Martha "did not feel as though her life was safe in [Washington's slaves'] hands."[8] She was worried slaves would try to kill her because their freedom depended upon her death. Only a year after her husband's death, Martha freed his slaves to relieve her anxiety. Many remained nearby, and as Washington's will had directed, a fund was set up to support young, old, and ill slaves. His heirs maintained it for more than 30 years. However, none of his family members followed his example in freeing the Custis slaves. Upon Martha's death, the slaves were divided among her heirs, and despite Washington's attempts to prevent it, many families were split.

Seen here with his personal attendant slave, Washington questioned slavery by the end of his life.

Chapter 10

How to Apply Moralist Criticism to Washington's Will

What Is Moralist Criticism?

Morality refers to the principles upon which a society bases its ideas of right and wrong. Moralist criticism, therefore, analyzes how a work presents right or wrong actions. Moral critics may analyze the characters or individuals in a work to determine whether they challenge or uphold society's moral code. In some cases, critics may also trace people's moral development, as they come to establish their own sense of right and wrong.

Applying Moralist Criticism to Washington's Will

Six months before he died in December 1799, George Washington finalized his will. In addition to typical provisions and bequests, the document also included a somewhat surprising clause: the emancipation of his slaves. Unfortunately, Washington left no explicit record in his will or other writings regarding why he chose to free his slaves. For years, scholars have debated the issue. But a close reading of his will and other documents, as well as a close look at historical evidence, may offer clues about his motivation. One can argue Washington's will reflects his moral development as he progresses from accepting slavery without question to doubting the morality of the institution.

To understand Washington's moral progression regarding slavery, one must first understand that for most of his life, he is a willing participant in the immoral system of slavery. In addition to inheriting slaves, he also purchases a number of slaves, including young women who

> **Thesis Statement**
> The thesis states: "One can argue Washington's will reflects his moral development as he progresses from accepting slavery without question to doubting the morality of the institution." In the essay, the author presents evidence of Washington's changing moral views regarding slavery.

> **Argument One**
> The author begins with the following argument: "To understand Washington's moral progression regarding slavery, one must first understand that for most of his life, he is a willing participant in the immoral system of slavery." This paragraph establishes how Washington's early views of slavery were in line with the morals of his day.

HOW TO APPLY MORALIST CRITICISM TO WASHINGTON'S WILL

bear slave children. As historian Henry Wiencek describes, Washington is "growing laborers as if they were a crop."[1] For many years, Washington does not hesitate to sell unwanted slaves, even if it means separating families. Like many slave owners, Washington takes minimal care of his slaves, and he gives explicit permission for his overseers to whip slaves when he deems it necessary. If slaves run away, Washington publicly offers rewards for their capture. Washington's behavior is in line with

In addition to questioning its morality, Washington perhaps also felt slavery was an inefficient form of farming.

87

How to Analyze the Works of **GEORGE WASHINGTON**

the Southern code of morality in which slaves are treated as mere property.

> **Argument Two**
> The author goes on to make the following argument: "After the American Revolution, however, Washington seems to become privately conflicted about slavery, although he does not acknowledge these feelings politically." This paragraph presents evidence of Washington's changing views on slavery.

<u>After the American Revolution, however, Washington seems to become privately conflicted about slavery, although he does not acknowledge these feelings politically.</u> To some extent, his emerging doubts are financially and politically motivated. In his letters, he states slavery is an inefficient and wasteful method of labor. In addition, he worries slavery has the potential to divide the North from the South and destroy the union. But evidence also suggests Washington is beginning to question slavery and its practices for moral reasons. By the mid-1770s, Washington makes it a practice not to separate families when buying and selling slaves. In 1779, he writes,

> If these poor wretches are to be held in a State of Slavery I do not see that a change of masters will render it more irksome, provided husband & wife, and Parents &

88

children are not separated from each other, which is not my intention to do.[2]

In private letters written later in 1794, Washington admits he possesses slaves "very repugnantly to my own feelings" and says he opposes selling slaves "as you would Cattle in the market."[3] At one time, he examines the possibility of selling land in order to finance freeing his slaves, but he never takes such a drastic step. Some scholars speculate Washington fears the political fallout, especially in the South, if the president emancipates his own slaves. In fact, as president, Washington does not publically share his opinions about slavery or take executive action against it. On the contrary, at times he seems to support it, such as when he signs the Fugitive Slave Act in 1793. His political and personal sentiments intersect, however, in a private letter from 1786, before he becomes president:

> *I can only say, that there is not a man living who wishes more sincerely than I do, to see a plan adopted for the abolition of it—but there is only one proper and effectual mode by which it can be accomplished, & that is*

How to Analyze the Works of **GEORGE WASHINGTON**

by Legislative authority; and this as far as my suffrage will go, shall never be wanting.[4]

> **Argument Three**
> The third argument states: "His will, then, in which he uses emotional yet practical language, is perhaps a reflection of his doubt at the end of his life about the morality of slavery." This argument analyzes how the will perhaps reveals Washington's moral view about slavery.

The year before his death, Washington tells a visitor he prays for an end to slavery "on the score of human dignity."[5] His will, then, in which he uses emotional yet practical language, is perhaps a reflection of his doubt at the end of his life about the morality of slavery. Although he "earnestly" wishes to free his slaves immediately upon his death, he fears doing so might split families and "excite the most painful sensations, if not disagreeable consequences."[6] As for the slave closest to him, Washington specifically addresses William Lee, granting him the special privilege of immediate freedom and a salary: "This I give him as a testimony of my sense of his attachment to me, and for his faithful services during the Revolutionary War."[7] Washington also acknowledges the practical consideration that some slaves will be too old or too young to support themselves upon emancipation. Washington writes, "it is my Will and desire that [they] shall be comfortably clothed & fed by my heirs while they live."[8] He makes special note of the orphans, who "are (by their Masters or Mistresses) to be taught to read & write; and to be brought up to some useful occupation."[9]

Washington also uses strong, forceful language regarding the emancipation of his slaves, perhaps because he understands his family does not hold the same views about slavery. His will explicitly directs his heirs regarding his slaves: "I do hereby expressly forbid the Sale . . . of any slave I may die possessed of, under any pretense whatsoever."[10] Further, he "most pointedly, and most solemnly" orders the executors of his will to "see that *this* clause respecting Slaves, and every part thereof be religiously fulfilled . . . without evasion, neglect or delay."[11] This language is quite commanding in comparison to the rest of the will. Such strong language indicates Washington is adamant his family must honor his wishes. It

> **Argument Four**
> In this paragraph, the author argues: "Washington also uses strong, forceful language regarding the emancipation of his slaves, perhaps because he understands his family does not hold the same views about slavery." With this argument, the author examines how Washington's commanding tone suggests his family does not see slavery as he does.

> **Conclusion**
> This final paragraph is the conclusion of the critique. It sums up the author's arguments and partially restates the original thesis. The conclusion also provides the reader with a new idea: Washington's views on slavery were ahead of his time.

perhaps also serves to preempt his family's objections, as he realizes they have not made the same moral progression he has regarding slavery.

With little known about his exact motives, historians debate why Washington frees his slaves in his will. One can argue he progresses from being a man who actively practices and upholds slavery to one who questions its political and economic value—and most importantly, its morality. If this is the case, then he is certainly ahead of his time. After his will, it will take more than half a century—and a civil war—before such a moral outlook leads to the abolition of slavery in the United States.

Thinking Critically about Washington's Will

Now it is your turn to assess the critique. Consider these questions:

1. The thesis argues that freeing his slaves in his will was a progression of Washington's moral development. Do you agree or disagree? Explain.

2. The author details how Washington does not take action against slavery publically, even after he begins to question it privately. Is enough evidence given to support this point?

3. Which argument is the weakest? How could it be made stronger?

Other Approaches

One way to apply moralist criticism to Washington's will is shown in the essay above. Two additional approaches are below. One example considers the possibility Washington does not make a moral progression regarding slavery. The other example focuses on Washington's desire to spread democratic values to America's youth.

Posthumous Freedom

Some scholars contend that although Washington freed his slaves in his will, he did not do so for moral reasons. Rather, they feel he was motivated by political or economic aims. They argue if Washington had been truly opposed to slavery for moral reasons, he would have freed his slaves during his lifetime. A thesis for a critique focusing on this could state: Although freeing his slaves may appear to be morally driven, Washington was more likely motivated by political and economic reasons that upheld the proslavery moral codes of his day.

Educational Pursuits

In his will, Washington left portions of his estate to build a university for continuing education in the United States. He states he is against the idea of young Americans traveling abroad for their education, where they may be indoctrinated with ideas contrary to the moral codes of democracy and liberty. A thesis addressing this might state: In providing funds to establish an American university, Washington sought to create an educational institution for the purpose of instilling young people with the moral system of a free, democratic nation.

You Critique It

Now that you have learned about different critical theories and how to apply them to different works, are you ready to perform your own critique? You have read that this type of evaluation can help you look at books, speeches, and essays in new ways and make you pay attention to certain issues you may not have otherwise recognized. So, why not use one of the critical theories profiled in this book to consider a fresh take on your favorite work?

First, choose a theory and the work you want to analyze. Remember that the theory is a springboard for asking questions about the work.

Next, write a specific question that relates to the theory you have selected. Then you can form your thesis, which should provide the answer to that question. Your thesis is the most important part of your critique and offers an argument about the work based on the tenets, or beliefs, of the theory you are applying. Recall that the thesis statement typically appears at the very end of the introductory paragraph of your essay. It is usually only one sentence long.

After you have written your thesis, find evidence to back it up. Good places to start are in the work itself or in journals or articles that discuss what other people have said about it. If you are critiquing a speech, you may also want to read about the speaker's life so you can get a sense of what factors may have affected the creation of the speech. This can be especially useful if working within historical or biographical criticism.

Depending on which theory you are applying, you can often find evidence in the work's language, structure, or historical context. You should also explore parts of the work that seem to disprove your thesis and create an argument against them. As you do this, you might want to address what other critics have written about the work. Their quotes may help support your claim.

Before you start analyzing a work, think about the different arguments made in this book. Reflect on how evidence supporting the thesis was presented. Did you find that some of the techniques used to back up the arguments were more convincing than others? Try these methods as you prove your thesis in your own critique.

When you are finished writing your critique, read it over carefully. Is your thesis statement understandable? Do the supporting arguments flow logically, with the topic of each paragraph clearly stated? Can you add any information that would present your readers with a stronger argument in favor of your thesis? Were you able to use quotes from the work, as well as from other critics, to enhance your ideas?

Did you see the work in a new light?

Timeline

1732 — George Washington is born on February 22.

1743 — Washington's father Augustine dies.

1748 — Washington joins a surveying trip to Virginia.

1749 — Washington is appointed surveyor in Culpeper County, Virginia.

1774 — Washington is elected as one of the Virginia representatives to the First Continental Congress.

1775 — During the Second Continental Congress, Washington is elected commander in chief of the Continental army; the American Revolution begins.

1783 — The Treaty of Paris ends the American Revolution; Washington resigns from his military career.

1789 — Washington is nominated as the first president of the United States; he delivers his first inaugural address on April 30.

How to Analyze the Works of **GEORGE WASHINGTON**

1752 After Washington's half-brother Lawrence dies, Washington inherits Mount Vernon; he is appointed as a military official.

1758 Washington resigns his military commission; he is elected to the House of Burgesses.

1759 Washington marries Martha Custis on January 6.

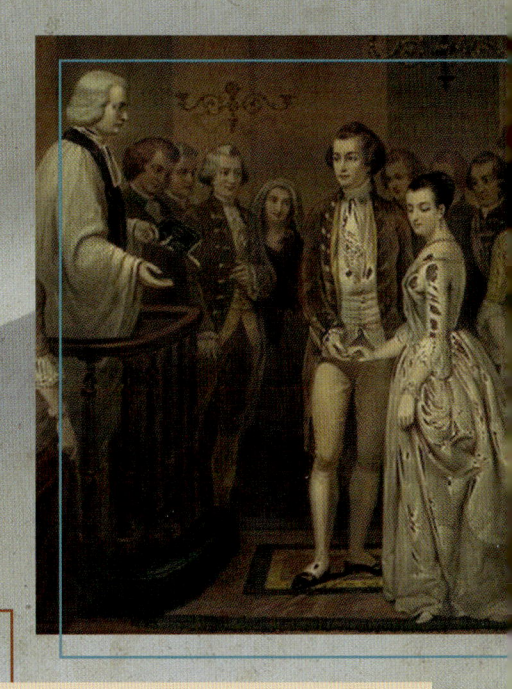

1793 Washington begins his second term as president.

1796 On March 21, Washington writes a letter of advice to his step-granddaughter about love and marriage; he publishes his Farewell Address on September 19.

1797 Washington's second term as president ends and he retires.

1799 Washington signs his last will and testament on July 9; on December 14, Washington dies at Mount Vernon.

99

Glossary

abolition
 The ending of a system, practice, or institution.

alliance
 A bond or connection.

coquettish
 Gaining the attention and admiration of men without sincere affection.

divisiveness
 Creating dissension, dividing.

dower
 The portion of an estate a widow receives upon her husband's death.

farewell
 A formal act of departure.

inaugural
 Marking a new beginning.

lament
   To express sorrow.

patriarchal
   Male-dominated.

patriotism
   Love of and devotion to one's country.

pecuniary
   Relating to money.

prudish
   Extreme modesty, primness.

surveyor
   A person who maps land.

Bibliography of Works and Criticism

Important Works

Speech to Officers at Newburgh, 1783

Circular to State Governments, 1783

Farewell Address to the Army, 1783

Letter to the President of the Continental Congress, 1787

Letter to the United Baptist Churches, 1789

First Inaugural Address, 1789

Letter to the Hebrew Congregation at Newport, 1790

Farewell Address, 1796

"Washington's Advice on Love & Marriage," 1796 (published 1861)

Last Will and Testament, 1799

Critical Discussions

Gedacht, Daniel. *George Washington: Leader of a New Nation*. New York: Rosen, 2004. Print.

McDonald, Forrest. *The American Presidency: An Intellectual History*. Lawrence, KS: Kansas UP, 1994. Print.

——. *The Presidency of George Washington*. Lawrence, KS: Kansas UP, 1974. Print.

Wood, Gordon S. *Empire of Liberty: A History of the Early Republic*. Oxford: Oxford UP, 2009. Print.

Resources

Selected Bibliography

Chernow, Ron. *Washington: A Life*. New York: Penguin, 2010. Print.

Henriques, Peter R. *Realistic Visionary: A Portrait of George Washington*. Charlottesville, VA: U of Virginia P, 2006. Print.

Randall, Willard Sterne, *George Washington: A Life*. New York: Henry Holt, 1997. Print.

Wiencek, Henry. *An Imperfect God: George Washington, His Slaves, and the Creation of America*. New York: Farrar, 2003. Print.

Further Readings

Earl, Sari K. *George Washington: Revolutionary Leader & Founding Father*. North Mankato, MN: ABDO, 2010. Print.

Unger, Harlow Giles. *The Unexpected George Washington: His Private Life*. Hoboken, NJ: John Wiley, 2006. Print.

Zall, Paul M. *Wit and Wisdom of the Founding Fathers: Benjamin Franklin, George Washington, John Adams, Thomas Jefferson*. New York: Ecco, 1996. Print.

Web Links

To learn more about critiquing the works of George Washington, visit ABDO Publishing Company online at **www.abdopublishing.com**. Web sites about the works of George Washington are featured on our Book Links page. These links are routinely monitored and updated to provide the most current information available.

For More Information

Historic Mount Vernon
3200 Mount Vernon Memorial Highway
Alexandria, VA 22309
703-780-2000
www.mountvernon.org

At Washington's estate, visitors can learn about the life of the first president.

University of Virginia, The Papers of George Washington
PO Box 400117, Charlottesville, VA 22904-4117
gwpapers.virginia.edu/index.html

The university maintains a compilation of Washington's documents and letters.

Source Notes

Chapter 1. Introduction to Critiques
None.

Chapter 2. A Closer Look at George Washington
1. Daniel Gedacht. *George Washington: Leader of a New Nation.* New York: Rosen, 2004. Print. 5.

Chapter 3. An Overview of Washington's First Inaugural Address
1. W. W. Abbot, ed. "The First Inaugural Address: Introduction." *The Papers of George Washington.* University of Virginia, 2011. Web. 8 Oct. 2012.
2. Ibid.
3. Ibid.
4. George Washington. "Washington's Inaugural Address of 1789: A Transcription." *National Archives.* The US National Archives and Records Administration, n.d. Web. 8 Oct. 2012.
5. Ibid.
6. Ibid.
7. Ibid.
8. Ibid.
9. Ibid.
10. Ibid.
11. Ibid.
12 Ibid.

Chapter 4. How to Apply Biographical Criticism to Washington's First Inaugural Address
1. "The Inauguration of George Washington, 1789." *EyeWitness to History.* Ibis Communications, Inc., 8 Oct. 2012. Web. 8 Oct. 2012.
2. George Washington. "Washington's Inaugural Address of 1789: A Transcription." *National Archives.* The US National Archives and Records Administration, n.d. Web. 8 Oct. 2012.
3. "The Inauguration of George Washington, 1789." *EyeWitness to History.* Ibis Communications, Inc., 8 Oct. 2012. Web. 8 Oct. 2012.
4. "George Washington Papers at the Library of Congress 1741–1799." *Library of Congress.* Library of Congress, 30 Aug. 2012. Web. 8 Oct. 2012.
5. George Washington. "Washington's Inaugural Address of 1789: A Transcription." *National Archives.* The US National Archives and Records Administration, n.d. Web. 8 Oct. 2012.

6. Ibid.
7. Ibid.
8. Ibid.
9. Ibid.
10. Ibid.

Chapter 5. An Overview of "Washington's Advice on Love & Marriage"

1. George Washington. "Washington's Advice on Love and Marriage: George Washington to Nelly Custis, 21 March 1796." *The Papers of George Washington*. University of Virginia, 2011. Web. 8 Oct. 2012.
2. Ibid.
3. Ibid.
4. Ibid.
5. Ibid.
6. Ibid.
7. Ibid.
8. Ibid.
9. Ibid.
10. Ibid.
11. Ibid.
12. Ibid.
13. Ibid.
14. Ibid.
15. Ibid.

Chapter 6. How to Apply Feminist Criticism to "Washington's Advice on Love & Marriage"

1. George Washington. "Washington's Advice on Love and Marriage: George Washington to Nelly Custis, 21 March 1796." *The Papers of George Washington*. University of Virginia, 2011. Web. 8 Oct. 2012.
2. Ibid.
3. Ibid.
4. Ibid.
5. Ibid.
6. Ibid.
7. Ibid.
8. Ibid.

Source Notes Continued

9. Ibid.
10. Ibid.
11. Ibid.
12. Ibid.

Chapter 7. An Overview of Washington's Farewell Address
1. George Washington. "George Washington's Farewell Address to the People of the United States." *Archiving Early America*. Archiving Early America, 2012. Web. 8 Oct. 2012.
2. Ibid.
3. Ibid.
4. Ibid.
5. Ibid.
6. Ibid.
7. Ibid.
8. Ibid.
9. Ibid.
10. Ibid.
11. Ibid.
12. Ibid.
13. Ibid.
14. Ibid.
15. Ibid.
16. Ibid.
17. Ibid.
18. Ibid.
19. Ibid.
20. Ibid.

Chapter 8. How to Apply Historical Criticism to Washington's Farewell Address
1. George Washington. "George Washington's Farewell Address to the People of the United States." *Archiving Early America*. Archiving Early America, 2012. Web. 8 Oct. 2012.
2. Ibid.
3. Ibid.
4. Ibid.
5. Ibid.
6. Ibid.
7. Ibid.
8. Ibid.

9. Ibid.
10. Ibid.
11. Ibid.

Chapter 9. An Overview of Washington's Will
1. George Washington. "The Will of George Washington Transcription" *The Papers of George Washington*. University of Virginia, 2011. Web. 8 Oct. 2012.
2. Ibid.
3. Ibid.
4. Ibid.
5. Ibid.
6. Ibid.
7. Ibid.
8. Ron Chernow. *Washington: A Life*. New York: Penguin, 2010. Print. 815.

Chapter 10. How to Apply Moralist Criticism to Washington's Will
1. Henry Wiencek. *An Imperfect God: George Washington, His Slaves, and the Creation of America*. New York: Farrar, 2003. Print. 121.
2. Dorothy Twohig. "That Species of Property: Washington's Role in the Controversy Over Slavery." *The Papers of George Washington*. University of Virginia, 2011. Web. 8 Oct. 2012.
3. Ibid.
4. Ibid.
5. Henry Wiencek. *An Imperfect God: George Washington, His Slaves, and the Creation of America*. New York: Farrar, 2003. Print. 352.
6. George Washington. "The Will of George Washington Transcription" *The Papers of George Washington*. University of Virginia, 2011. Web. 8 Oct. 2012.
7. Ibid.
8. Ibid.
9. Ibid.
10. Ibid.
11. Ibid.

Index

American Daily Advertiser, 58
American Revolution, 16–18, 41, 70
Ames, Fisher, 24
arguments, how to write, 10, 96–97

Bank of the United States, 18
Barbados, 14–15
Battle of Long Island, 16–17
biographical criticism, 7–9, 29–39
  conclusion, 36
  evidence and arguments, 30–36
  other approaches, 38–39
  thesis statement, 30
Britain, 16–17, 39, 65, 69, 79

colonies, 15, 16, 66
Congress, US, 23, 25–26, 35–36
Constitution, US, 18, 25–26, 30, 35, 57, 61, 73
Constitutional Convention, 17, 73
Continental army, 16
critical theory, definitions of, 6–9
  biographical, 29
  feminist, 47
  historical, 65
  moralist, 85
Custis, Daniel Parke, 76
Custis, Eleanor "Nelly," 41–45, 48–55, 81
Custis, George "Washy," 41, 42
Custis, John, 15, 41
Custis, Patsy, 41

Dandridge, Bartholomew, 80
Dandridge, Mary, 80–81
Delaware River, 17
District of Columbia, 79

Electoral College, 18
evidence, how to use, 10, 96–97

Fairfax, Lord, 14
Fairfax, Sally, 42
Farewell Address, 20, 57–63, 65–73
Federalist Party, 20, 67
feminist theory, 47–55
  conclusion, 52
  evidence and arguments, 48–52
  other approaches, 54–55
  thesis statement, 48
First Continental Congress, 16
first inaugural address, 18, 23–27, 29–39
French and Indian War, 15
Fugitive Slave Act, 89

George Washington University, 79–80

Hamilton, Alexander, 57, 67
historical criticism, 65–73
  conclusion, 70
  evidence and arguments, 66–70
  other approaches, 72–73
  thesis statement, 66
House of Burgesses, 15, 16

Jefferson, Thomas, 67

Lee, Henry, 21
Lee, William, 78–79, 90
Lewis, Lawrence, 45

Maclay, William, 24
Madison, James, 57
moralist criticism, 85–95
   conclusion, 92
   evidence and arguments,
     86–92
   other approaches, 94–95
   thesis statement, 86
Mount Vernon, 15, 20, 76, 80, 81

New York, 17–18, 23, 31

Philadelphia, 18
political parties, 20, 30, 60–61,
   67–69

questions, critical thinking, 37,
   53, 71, 93

Recollections of Washington, 42
Republican Party, 20, 67

Second Continental Congress, 16
Senate, US, 70
Siege of Boston, 16
slavery, 13, 20, 30, 75–79,
   80–81, 82–83, 85–95
surveying, 14

thesis statement, how to write,
   9, 96–97
Treaty of Paris, 18

Virginia, 13, 14, 15, 16, 17, 75, 80

Washington, Augustine, 13, 14,
   32, 38, 39, 76
Washington, Bushrod, 81
Washington, George,
   early life, 13–14
   later life, 20–21
   marriage and family, 15
   military career, 15, 16–18
   presidency, 18–20
Washington, Lawrence, 13, 14,
   15
Washington, Martha Dandridge
   Custis, 15, 20, 41, 42, 43,
   76–77, 80, 82–83
Washington, Mary Ball, 13
Washington DC, 18
"Washington's Advice on Love
   and Marriage," 41–45, 47–55
Washington's will, 20, 75–83,
   95–95
Whiskey Rebellion, 19

United States of America, 13,
   18–19, 23, 29, 35, 36, 38, 39,
   65, 69, 70, 72, 79, 82, 92, 95

Yorktown, 18

About the Author

Annie Qaiser is a freelance writer. She lives in Saint Paul, Minnesota, with her husband and children.

Photo Credits

Gilbert Stuart, cover, 3; Getty Images/ThinkStock, 12, 98 (top); North Wind/North Wind Picture Archives, 17, 22, 28, 34, 50, 56, 64, 78, 84; Brand X Pictures/ThinkStock, 21; Henry S Sadd//Library of Congress, 27, 98 (bottom); Bettmann/Corbis / AP Images, 40; Junius Brutus Stearns/Library of Congress, 45, 74, 87, 99; Anna W. Betts/Library of Congress, 46; iStockPhotos/ThinkStock, 63; Francis Miller/Time Life Pictures/Getty Images, 68